TANGLEWOODS

THE ANETHUNDER
SCHOOL FOR FAMILIARS

FRANGETOWN

First Terrestrial
Witches' Bank

HORIZON LINE

TO THE OTHERSIDE

D0582951

Rumblewick's ~~MY~~ DIARY ⑤

My Unwilling ~~MY~~ WITCH flies high

Hiawyn Oram ✳ Sarah Warburton

ORCHARD BOOKS

A SHORT HISTORY
OF HOW YOU COME TO BE READING MY
VERY PRIVATE DIARIES

In a snail shell, they were STOLEN. Oh yes, no less. My witch Haggy Aggy (HA for short) sneaked into my log basket and helped herself.

According to her, this is what happened:

On one of her many shopping trips to Your Side she met a Book Wiz. (I am told you call them publishers, though Wiz seems more fitting as they make books appear, as if by magic, every day of the week.)

Anyway, this Book Wiz/publisher wanted HA to write an account of HER life as a witch here on Our Side. Of course, HA wasn't willing to do that. Being the most unwilling witch in witchdom, she is far too busy shopping, watching telly, not cackling, being anything BUT a witch and getting me into trouble with the High Hags* as a result.

The Book Wiz begged on her knees (apparently) and offered HA a life's supply of shoes if she came up with something. So HA did. She came up with THIS — MY DIARIES. ALL OF THEM!!!!

Of course, when I wrote the diaries, I was not expecting anyone to read them. Let alone Othersiders like you. But as you are, here is a word to the wise about how things work between us:

* The High Hags run everything round here. They RULE.

1. We are here on THIS SIDE and you are there on the OTHER SIDE.

2. Between us is the HORIZON LINE.

3. You don't see we're here, on This Side, living our lives, because for you the HORIZON LINE is always a day away. You can walk for a thousand moons (or more for all I know), but you'll never reach it.

4. On the other paw, we know you're there because we visit you all the time. This is partly because of broomsticks. A broomstick has no trouble with any Horizon Line anywhere. A broomstick (with one or more of us upon it) just flies straight through.

And it has to be like that because scaring Otherside children into their wits is part of witches' work. In fact it is Number One on the Witches' Charter of Good Practice (see copy glued at the back).

On the other paw, it is NOWHERE in the Charter for a witch to go over to Your Side to make friends and try to be and do everything you are and do — as my witch Haggy Aggy does.

But then, that's my giant problem: being cat to a witch who doesn't want to be one. And as you will see from these diaries, it makes my life a right BAG OF HEDGEHOGS. So all I can say is, if HA tries to make friends with YOU, send her straight back to This Side with a spider in her ear.

Thank you,

Rumblewick Spellwacker Mortimer B. xxx

This Diary Belongs to:

Rumblewick Spellwacker Mortimer B.

RUMBLEWICK for short, RB for shortest

Nearest Otherside Telephone:
Ditch and Candleberry Bush Street,
N by SE Over the Horizon

Birth Day:
Windy Day 23rd Magogary

Education:
The Awethunder School For Familiars
12-Moon Apprenticeship to the
High Hag Witch Trixie Fiddlestick

Qualifications:
Certified Witch's Familiar

Current Employment:
Seven-year contract with Witch Hagatha Agatha,
Haggy Aggy for short, HA for shortest

Hobbies:
Cathastics, Point-to-Point Shrewing, Languages

Next of Kin:
Uncle Sherbet (retired Witch's Familiar)
Mouldy Old Cottage,
Flying Teapot Street,
Prancetown

Fright Full Warning Night

Dear Diary,

All right — we know she's unwilling.
We know she'd rather be a ballet dancer
or a supermodel or a star cheffer on
Otherside TV. But now she's gone into
orbit on the matter.

Yesterday, I'd been to catnastics with
Grimey — and got home to find her holding
a Broomstick Shed Sale.

All our best broomsticks were out on
display. She was selling them to Familiars in
exchange for names of children who'd been
frightened by their witches — so she could
go and COMFORT the little ratlets!

Now, it's me who tunes our broomsticks. Me who lovingly keeps them in perfect flying trim — and there she was just about GIVING THEM AWAY!

I'm sorry, but on this occasion, I failed to be respectful.

"What are you DOING?"

I yelled, snatching the best wind-cutter I've ever ridden from the paws of Arbuthnot Butnot (Witch Rattle's Familiar). "WE need our broomsticks. Every one of them!"

"I don't," HA replied, tossing her hair like the supermodel she longs to be. "As you well know, I get broomstick sick just looking at a broomstick."

I ask you as I've asked before. What kind of a witch gets broomstick sick? Mine. But here's the thing, Diary:

ONLY WHEN IT SUITS HER.

When she WANTS to,

when she NEEDS to,

she hops a broomstick without a hint

of the bellycobbles.

Anyway, losing some of our best-tuned broomsticks was only the start of it.

As I was shutting what was left of them in the shed, I reminded her she should get ready for the Full Moon Cackling Competition up at High Hags HQ.

"Cackling competition, RB?" she screeched.

"You should know by now, I do not go in for such cacophonous collywash. So say goodbye to that subject."

Only it wasn't goodbye to that subject.

This morning the High Hag Dame Amuletta came round to find out why she hadn't been crawing with the rest of them.

HA spotted her land hair-first in the bushes. (What a rubble broomstick rider that Hag is!)

"Quick," she ordered.

"Make me invisible.

At the triple presto,

before she sees

I'm home."

So I did, using the Tried and Tested
Out-Of-Sight Spell learned in first
grade. Then — even as she was fading from
view — she ordered, "Say you're inventing
a new Invisiblising Spell which you tried out
on me — only to find the Reversal Clause
doesn't work...that's why I wasn't at the
Cackling Do because someone who isn't
anywhere can't be somewhere
cackling in a... (She'd faded.)

So that's what I told Amuletta when she poked her nose into every corner of 13 Chimneys looking for HA.

And immediately wished I hadn't.

Because she threw a fit – complete with

FRIGHT FULL

WARNING.

"Rumblewick Spellwacker Mortimer B," she fizzed, "The other High Hags and I are up to our hats with you failing in your duty to keep your witch in the ways of Proper Practice. You were such a promising Familiar when you were apprenticed to Fiddlestick. We had high hopes of you — and now where are you? Well, answer me?"

"Uh...cat to a witch who...uh..." I muttered.

"Cat to a witch who uh, because you let her get away with it. A witch who uh isn't uh visible because you can't invent a spell with a reliable reversal clause! Have you forgotten EVERYTHING you learned at Awethunder's?

Because if you have, we'll have you back there in a split trice! Now get poor Hagatha back in sight SOMEHOW. I DON'T CARE HOW. And then inform her we have a Child-Scaring Jaunt tomorrow — gathering at HQ at Three Hours Before Children's Bedtime.

I want her there and visible.

And if she isn't,

I'll be wagging my pointing finger

AT YOU.

Thank you and good spelling."

As soon as she was gone, I reversed the Out of Sighter and looked at HA with a 'well, do you want me to be sent back to Awethunder's or WHAT' long and hard look.

It was like slime off a frog's back.

"Oh RB, don't take that old Hag so seriously," she laughed. "She talks such grubspittle. She'd never send you back to school. And one thing I can tell you is this — I'm NOT going child-scaring tomorrow.

Why? Because

1 child-scaring is pifflefluff
and out of the Dark Ages and
2 the last episode of Catwalk is on TV
and I'm not missing it for anything."

Impossible or what?

Anyway, I'll go on later.
Right now I have
to work out
how to get
her on this
child-scaring
jaunt — or
I'm a first grader.

It Backfires But The Hags Are Impressed Day Night

Dear Diary,

How things turn out in ways you couldn't predict if you tried for thirteen moons: I've just been to the Other Side to the house of a ratlet called Ameline Amethirst. To drop in three 'free tickets' for a giant treat at the Giant Tent also known as the Circus. How come? I'll do my best to explain.

I got HA to go on the Child-Scaring Jaunt by finding out that the last episode of Catwalk was on before the Gathering Hour for the Jaunt — so she couldn't use that as an excuse.

Then I suggested she join in the Jaunt so she could be right there on the spot to comfort the children who'd been frightened.

Her eyes lit up like giant glow worms. "Now you're thinking, RB! Any ideas on HOW I might do that right there on the spot?"

"Of course," I said. "I've invented this AT-THE-CLICK-OF-MY-FINGERS-I'M-A-SILLY-DOGLET SPELL. You see, for some reason all children love silly doglets. They are mightily comforted by the running round in circles and the slappy face-licking that silly doglets do. So, as soon as you see a child has been terrified, just become a silly doglet and you'll bring comfort on the spot."

"You are a brilliant Familiar and you are mine though I say it myself," said HA.

"So fly me to the Gathering Point for this Child...er... Comforting Jaunt!"

Very silly

Funny silly

Big silly

Long thin silly

Frilly silly

Please note, no mention of  broomstick sickness now and for your info here is the SILLY DOGLET SPELL.

AT-THE-CLICK-OF-MY-FINGERS-I'M-A-SILLY-DOGLET SPELL

Pull hat down to your chin, click heels five times in counter rhythm to five finger clicks while chanting:

A doglet I am, a doglet you see
The silliest doglet that ever could be
I circle, I tumble, I jump in a lap
I chase and I puddle, I lick and I yap
A sillier doglet — now all will agree —
There never has been — than the doglet that's me!

Reversal: To reverse this spell presto, turn five circles with your silly doglet tail in your teeth while yapping between tail-clenched teeth, YIP, YAP, YAPPITTY YAP. Repeat five times.

I'll go on later — HA is deciding what to wear to the Tent Event with Ameline and friends tomorrow and she wants me to help choose her shoes??

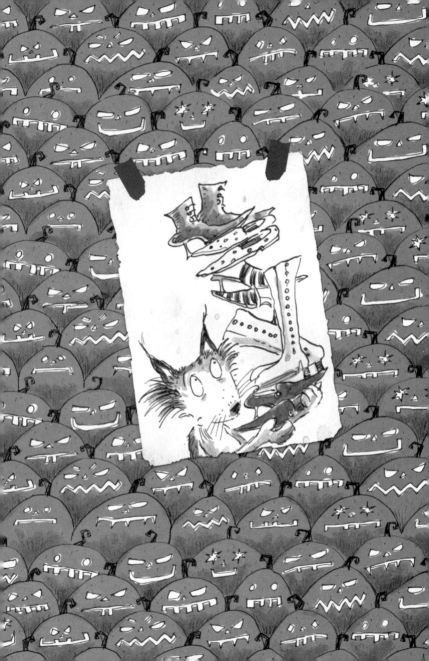

Dear Diary,

I don't know why she does that. Whatever shoes I pick out, she wears the ones she wants to wear anyway.

So where was I? Oh yes. Silly doglets and joining the Jaunt. Amuletta was thrilled to see us fly up at the appointed Gathering Hour. Especially as HA seemed so keen to get going — which she was — though little did Amuletta know, it was to comfort, not to scare!

Once we'd crossed the Horizon Line, Amuletta ordered us to split into smaller Scaring Parties — some to go This Way, some That Way and HA and me to go Down The Mall — with her!

And here's where we first met Ameline Amethirst and her two friends!!

They were in an Eaterie — stuffing themselves with blurgers and chups (or whatever that favourite Otherside grubspittle is called).

"Watch this and learn,"

Amuletta hissed as she turned herself into a Look-Alike Table Clearer to turn Ameline and friends' blurgers and chups into frog in slime buns and roasty cutworms!!

Duly terrified, the ratlets started screaming and cowering — losing their appetites and getting the bellycobbles

big-o-time.

But HA was right there with my Silly Doglet Spell.

Only, she didn't remember that doglets don't talk as in talk — they yap. And once a silly doglet, she ran round in silly circles, jumped into Ameline's lap and SPOKE.

And KEPT ON SPEAKING as follows:
"Oh precious children, don't be afraid.
It was only some old Hag who believes it's
her mission to scare you into your wits.
I suppose she thinks blurgerburbers and
chups are bad for you. Well, maybe they
are. But that's no reason to terrify you.
Now, you listen to me. I'll be here to
comfort you even if you get scared by all
the witches in witchdom."

Well, Ameline and friends were frightened
before, but now, having a doglet
    in their laps, speaking to them in words
as clear as larksong — they
        were gripped with
hysteria and swooning.

"Dog...bewitched...it... speaks!" cried Ameline before she fell in a flat swoon and grown Othersiders came running — to cure her, catch the frogs and chase HA the talking doglet out of their Eaterie.

Outside, once HA had reversed the spell and was herself again, she was all for going back in and

EXPLAINING EVERYTHING.

But at that moment Amuletta came up as herself — TO CONGRATULATE HA — for causing scariness so great it brought on hysteria and swooning!!! "You flintspark of a proper practising witch!" cackled Amuletta. "And whose idea was the talking doglet?"

"HIS!" HA almost sobbed — pointing at me. (She was very distressed at the way things were turning out.)

"Then congratulations to you, RB," Amuletta cackled. "My fright full warning must have worked. And how mightily relieved I am to see you turning over a new twig."

So do you see what I mean about things going in directions no one could have predicted? All I'd cared about was getting HA to go on the Child-Scaring Jaunt.

What I was not expecting was HA completely terrifying some ratlets — by mistake — and thereby getting <u>ME</u> saved from being sent back to Familiar School in disgrace!

Anyway, I could see HA was close to tears for all the terrifying she'd done through her forgetfulness of the ways of doglets.

So I got her excused from the rest of the Jaunt.

"Turning yourself into a silly doglet,"

I put it to Amuletta,

"completely knocks the witchways out of you.

She must be allowed to rest."

"I can see that, RB," cackled Amuletta. "Now you be a faithful Familiar and fly her home at once."

Only HA refused to go home until I'd helped her find a way to make it up to the 'girls'.

We sat on a bench in the nearby grassy green patch to think of how. As always I had the only gemmy idea.

"Give them a treat," I said.

"A giant treat."

"Such as?" snivelled HA. "What is a giant treat to girls like the Amelines?"

I stared out at the grassy green around us and the giant tent in the middle of it. There were ratlets and their growns walking around outside the tent. Many of them were holding coloured bobblers on strings and putting their tongues into clouds of frothy pink lichen which they seemed to find pleasing. All looking plump with treatedness.

"Be back in a few streaks of a broomstick," I said, and went to investigate.

What I found when I peeked inside that giant tent was this:

A circle of sawdust in the middle of it. Ratlets and growns sitting in seats around the circle, awe-breathing with delight as...into the sawdust circle came Giant Othersiders — five broomsticks end-on-end high.

They juggled coloured balls, faster and faster. Then half-sized themselves and quarter-sized themselves — but all the time they kept on juggling those balls — higher and faster — and never a one went askew.

Next some normal-sized Othersiders
came into the circle — while music played
to get you rump-wriggling on your seat.
And they seemed to juggle themselves. They
bounced into the air — onto each others'
shoulders, higher and higher — until they'd
made a giant honeybee comb, and
dismantled the comb by juggling themselves
back into the air. All without one of them
going askew.

I was spellbound and could tell by
the ratlets' gawping and shining
eyes that I'd stumbled on

Giant Treat Land!!

I sped back to HA, who was trying to make friends with a ratlet and her grown, called her away and gave her the good news. "That," I said,

"is the Giant Treat you're looking for."

HA stared. "But what would the Amelines want with a tent?"

"No, no," I explained. "You don't give them the tent. You get them tickets to go and watch what goes on inside the tent. It is called a Circus — I've read the signs — it's mightily awe-striking and tickets may be had right there at that brightly-coloured houselet."

And that leads me to where I was when I told you I'd got back from delivering the Circus tickets. HA thought my Giant Treat idea was completely IT. She bought five tickets on her Shopalot Card and I slipped three through the Ameline letter box with a note HA had dictated.

(The other two tickets are ours.)

The HA-dictated note said:

These **FREE** tickets are for you and
your friends to go to the Circus on the
green patch not far from your house
TOMORROW AFTERNOON. I am giving
them to you as a Giant Treat

because you were so scared by that talking
doglet some silly witch turned herself into.
Please be comforted by this
Giant Treat and see you there.

Yours —
Hagatha Agatha
(not the witch who willingly
did that to you)

Right, that's it for now.

HA is demanding I chef up some TV-watching snacklets and hey-press her dress in readiness for tomorrow — and somewhere between all this and then

I've got to get some shut-eye!!

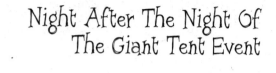

Night After The Night Of The Giant Tent Event

Dear Diary,

Oh sorry day I poked my nose inside a Circus Tent. Sorry, sorry day. Do you know where HA and I spent most of last night? No and you probably don't want to know. But as you are my Diary you just have to hear it.

We spent it in what is known on the Other Side as a Police Cell. And all I can say is do not get yourself into a Police Cell if you can help it because it is not an easy place to get out of.

This is how it went:

We arrived at the Circus and took our seats. Ameline and friends did NOT join us — which meant HA was so disappointed she could hardly focus on the juggling in the sawdust circle.

I did though. My Lucky Whisker went
straight with awe while she fretted about
the Amelines missing their Giant Treat

UNTIL...

with a tirra tirra on the drums...into the
sawdust ring came the HIGH FLYERS or
TRAPEZE ARTISTS as they are
also called over there.

Oh my Lucky
Whisker. Oh my long
line of familial
Familiars.

*I WISH YOU
COULD HAVE SEEN
WHAT THEY CAN DO* — flying
through the air with the greatest of
ease — no magic, no broomsticks

(that we could see anyway).

NOW HA focussed. How she focussed.
She gasped and gawed more than any
of the ratlets.

And even though those trapeze high
flyers hadn't anywhere near finished their
act, she stood up clapping and screeching:

"Supernova,
supernova,

look at
that – no
magic, no
broomsticks!"

And that's when it all started to go screw-wiggle — and a thick black arrow leading straight to POLICE CELL might just as well have appeared over our heads.

Police cell

HA called out to the Flyers — startling
them as they flew between their
fast-swinging trapezes — "Hold on!
I have to join you.
                    I have to do it too!"
  Then to me, "RB, pass me our
fold-away. Because I'm up there.
I'm going to fly high."
  Now I gawed at her, thinking

    SOCKS, SOCKS,

TADPOLES IN SOCKS,

HERE WE GO

AND TRIPLE

HELP!

I did not reach under my seat for our fold-away. I just exploded: "If you want to fly high, you can, anytime. On Our Side. Across the wide open skies. On a broomstick. Where You Belong!"

"Rubble!" she hissed. "This is where I belong. I see it for now. I see it for the future. Me — the starriest-spangled, highest flyer ever. Gaining the awe of children everywhere — right here in the Circus. Now, give me that broomstick!"

"**No!**" I said, tucking
my paws away so they
were not tempted to obey.

"Not in a million moons."

But HA never takes no for an answer. She dived for it herself, jumped onto her seat and mounted it!

Well, by now we were causing such a commotion, the trapeze flyers were standing on their high platforms or swinging quietly on their trapezes, gawping at us (as was the WHOLE audience).

Down in the sawdust circle, the other
Circus Othersiders were running around
in circles, dragging out what
looked like a giant net.

I made one

last ditch attempt

to get HA to

SIT DOWN.

"Remember your broomstick sickness. And you're not DRESSED for it. You have to be dressed for it!"

"And I soon will be!

Watch me!" she laughed as she rose straight and true into the air to make for the heights of the Tent — where swung those trapezes.

A giant OHHHH from the audience rose with her.

A two-giant
OHHHH – AHHHH
was exhaled
as she landed neatly
on the bar of an empty trapeze,
nearly lost her balance – didn't – but

<u>DID</u> let go of our broomstick!!!

I watched in despair as it fell, folding itself neatly (tuned to do so) — thinking only, _no broomstick, _no way home!

And, not caring whose heads I leapt over — I bounded through the audience, trying to foretell where it would land.

With half an eye I thought I saw it hit the sawdust. Couldn't be sure because the other eye and a half were distracted by the commotion HA was causing.

She was standing on the trapeze — without magic, without broomstick — about to fly!!

Down in the sawdust ring,
the Chief Circusmaker was shouting,

"NET, NET, NET"

to the Circus workers and

"NO! NO! NO!" up at HA.

The Chief High Flyer, who had skimmed
down a pole to talk to the Chief
Circusmaker, was now skimmying back up
to try and reach HA. And all the time, he
was shouting,

"NO! NO! NO!
You do not do that.
You are not trained.
You must not do it!"

"YES, YES, YES, I must do it,"
she called back.

"All I need is star-spangles."

With that, she flipped
off her hat with one
flick of her pointing
finger and sent
it skimming
through the air towards a girl
High Flyer standing on a platform.
As it skimmed, she screeched,

"All you wear with stars and spangles,

Glittering garments,
nets and bangles,

Now upon this word

RAT-TAT,

Flies to me inside my hat!"

Witch without
a broomstick!!!

Triple yikes!!

To everyone's dedazzlement (excepting mine because I know what a great witch she is when she wants to be) the girl High Flyer was instantly wearing nothing but her swim-wear. Because her costume was winging its way back to HA — in the hat.

I don't think anyone saw exactly how HA did the next thing because it happened in the blink of an eye, but now the costume was OUT of the hat and ON HA — and HA's clothes were in a neat pile down below in the sawdust circle!!!

The Chief Circusmaker and the Chief High Flyer froze, their faces white as frost.

Some ratlets and
growns in the audience cheered.

Some SCREAMED. Some growns put their
hands over their ratlets' eyes. Some tried to
run from the Tent.

While, high above them, star-spangled
and loving it, HA worked her trapeze til it
was swinging wildly.

Then, crying, "Look! No magic,
no broomstick, no training,
just star-spangles!"

she threw herself into the nothing and
no-holding of air — roughly in the
direction of another trapeze.

For one trice,

I admit,

she looked as if

she was flying.

But then, in less than thirteen trices,

she began to plumdrop!

And as she began to drop, all my moons as her Familiar **tumbled** before my eyes. I re-saw the good times and the <u>worst</u>.

I forgave her all her unwillingness. I forgave her wearing pink.

Hiding her black.

Loving frogs

and getting me <u>disgraced</u>.

At the same time knowing — if I was any kind of Familiar — I'd be summoning our broomstick from the dust and winging it to her. I'd be inventing a reverse plumdrop spell in the split tricelet available. Or at the very least a spell to land her softly.

Instead, stone-petrified at the thought
I was about to lose the only witch I had,
I DID NOTHING.

And THEN...

I saw,
she didn't need me
to save her.

witchless

The GIANT Net
was being hoisted up and the
Chief High Flyer was flying out to
catch her.

With one arm, he swept her out of fall's
way. With the other arm he caught a stray
trapeze, swung it, waited, swung it and
dropped…using himself to cushion her
landing in the net.

Well, you'd think she'd have showered
him with flowers of thanks. But not my
Haggy Aggy. Oh no. Not my witch.

White, she went. Then green, puce — the
sure sign a fit is coming on.

Lying in the net she shrieked,
"WHY? WHY? You spoilt it all.
I was flying high!"

She pointed her pointing
finger at him. No doubt to
spell him to sawdust
or finer.

And that
was when THE ARROW
pointing straight to THE POLICE CELL
tipped the top of her head.

There was ear-splitting wailing. The giant net had been lowered to the ground and into the sawdust circle came running POLICE CELLERS!!!

Catching her by surprise, they untangled her from the net, marched her out of the Tent — and bundled her into a wailing motor.

They slammed the motor's door before I could leap in beside her, which meant a very scary ride for me — all the way to their Station — clinging to the flashing screaming wailer on the motor's roof!

In fact, just thinking about
that ride makes me so dizzy,

I must curl up

and take a few tads

of soothing shut-eye.

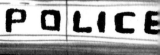

Dear Diary,

It's me.

I'm back. De-dizzified enough to go on. And here I go. At the Police Cellers' Station, they 'cautioned' Haggy Aggy against saying anything (tadpole-size chance of that).

Then they 'charged' her with 'making a Public Disturbance'!! Marched her to a Cell. Wouldn't let me in with her (though she threatened to turn them into fat pumpkins if they didn't) AND LOCKED THE DOOR.

Luckily — as it would turn out — there was a small opening in the door for talking through. Immediately HA was at it talking — even though she'd been 'cautioned' not to.

"You've rubbled everything, you Othersiders!" she yelled.

"I've waited all my lives to fly high in a star-spangled costume and get the precious children gawing with excitement."

The Police Cellers ignored her. They'd turned their attention to catching me (no doubt with the intention of putting me in Cat Prison). But I was quicker than them. At the triple presto I turned myself into a FLY ON THE WALL — so I could creep through the Talking Hole in the cell door to comfort HA.

"I'm here," I buzzed.

"No, not there.

Here on this wall.

Now, will you please calm down and together we'll get you home."

"I don't want to go home," she pouted. "I want to spangle and fly high."

"But HA," I buzzed as soothingly as anyone can buzz. "You are not trained to spangle and fly high without magic or a broomstick."

"Then I'll do it <u>WITH</u> magic and a broomstick!" she yelled.

"Just give me a chance!"

Even as she spoke, an idea came to me. "As soon as we are home," I buzzed, "we'll stage our own flying-high show. Up in the open skies where we belong. We'll take up some broomsticks. Hang swings from them. Invite everyone from Wizton and around. And you — in your star-spangles — can awe them with your trapezery work.

It wasn't easy. Partly because she wasn't thinking in a straight line.

She still wanted to settle the score with the Police Cellers for snatching her from the Giant Tent Event.

She went to the Talking Hole and yelled until two Cellers came running. She said,

"Let me out of here NOW or I'll turn you into mice with three tails."

They didn't let her out so she did. And when more Cellers came running she warned them to let her out or she'd turn them into

mice with three heads.

And when even more came she
turned them into

singing beetles,
bats with green fangs,
smoking chimneys,
and walking
witches' hats.

I eventually got her to stop and listen,
"HA, you can turn all the Cellers in the
universe into whatever you want — but
that will not get you out of here."

"Well then we'd better spell up the key,
RB," she pouted. "That can't be beyond us."

But it was — though not for want of
trying. We spelled up 37 keys.

None of them turned the
lock and let us free.

So there we sat — well,
she sat and I crawled — with
all our
powers.
Stuck.

Then I had the Last Chance idea.

"Start yelling through the Talking Hole again. They'll send more Cellers from somewhere. But before they arrive, I'll make you invisible using the Tried and Trusted Out of Sighter. Then, as far as they can see, YOU ARE NOT HERE. AND THEY'LL OPEN THE DOOR. Because what is the point of locking up nothing but emptiness? NO POINT

AT ALL.

As soon as the door is open, you walk out invisibly and I crawl out on the walls."

"Glittery, RB.

Totally glittery!" HA beamed. "What would I do without you? Let's get to it."

It wasn't that simple. I had to turn myself back to myself in order to perform the Out of Sighter. But there wasn't time to get back to Fly on Wall mode before two more Cellers arrived in response to HA's yells.

Let me out or I'll call the POLICE!

They did open the door — in great puzzlement — seeing only a cat in the cell and no Haggy Aggy.

She walked free — invisible as she was — but now they came for ME!

Luckily, as the door was open, I was able to avoid them by streaking through it and melting into the crowd that filled the corridor. Result? I strolled out of that Police Cellers' Station, neatly disguised as one of the crowd — under a *witch's* *hat!*

But once free, and I'd discarded the disguise and re-in-sighted HA, our problems were nowhere near over.

We had to get back home —

OVER THE

HORIZON LINE

— and we didn't have

a broomstick!!

We tried calling Grimey 73 times from an Otherside Telephone but each time all we got was a strange Othersider voice saying,

"Sorry-the-number-you-have-dialled-has-not-been-recognised-please-try-again."

So we decided to risk going back to the Circus to look for our fold-away. When at last we found the Giant Tent (everything looks different in the dark on the Other Side) it was empty. And, thank my Lucky Whisker, there it was — lying ignored in the sawdust, looking more like a sad stick than the finely tuned broomstick it is!

HA was so relieved, she offered to fly us home herself — with no mention of

broomstick sickness!!

86

As for any further interest in trapezery, well, as soon as I set about organising her flying-high act in the open skies, she went pale and quiet.

And when I told her I was off to invite all and sundry in Wizton to come and enjoy it — she was already out of the star-spangled costume, into her dressing gown and watching TV.

"OH RB," she sighed.

"I'd do it, of course.
          I'd star-spangle them.

But what is the point in stunning witches
and hags and Familiars?
It's the precious children that need

the treat of it. So don't bother for now
and besides...you know how sick I feel
even at the thought of a broomstick."

I didn't argue.
Didn't say
a word.

Just picked up
the star-spangled costume she'd
dropped — packed it into her flying
trunk and sent it winging its way back
to the Circus where it belongs!

Thank you for listening,
Diary, and good night!

2 Useful Spells for your Info:

SPELL TO TURN YOURSELF INTO A FLY ON THE WALL IN A TRIPLE PRESTO

Cross your legs, knot your tail and curl your Lucky Whisker three times to the left while chanting under your breath:

In a flash, in this moment, I cannot be me
I cannot be noticed at all
By the time I've said trice not once but thrice thrice,
I am but a fly on the wall
BUZZ BUZZ!

Small Print and Reversal: No time for small print.
To reverse, knot your legs (front and back), flap
wings three times at double presto and chant the
spell-chant backwards.

THE TRIED AND TRUSTED SPELL TO OUT-OF-SIGHT YOUR WITCH FOR HER OWN GOOD

Make a breeze by sneezing seven times.
Curl your Lucky Whisker backwards and chant:

It's in your own interest
That you're out of sight
So wherever you are
There is nothing but light,
Not an arm or a thumb
Not a leg or a tum
Not one scrap or one cell
Though you're perfectly well
Not a hair in between
When this spell is said
CAN BE SEEN!

WITCHES' CHARTER
OF GOOD PRACTICE

1. Scare at least one child on the Other Side
into his or her wits – every day (excellent),
once in seven days (good), once a moon (average),
once in two moons (bad), once in a blue
moon (failed).

2. Identify any fully-grown Othersiders who
were not properly scared into their wits as
children and DO IT NOW. (It is never too
late for a grown Othersider to come to
his or her senses.)

3. Invent a new spell useful for every purpose and
every occasion in the Witches' Calendar.
Ensure you or your Familiar commits it to
a Spell Book before it is lost to the
Realms of Forgetfulness for ever.

4. Keep a proper witch's house at all
times – filled with dust and spiders' webs, mould
and earwigs underthings and ensure the jars on
your kitchen shelves are always alive with
good spell ingredients.

5. Cackle a lot. Cackling can be heard far and wide and serves many purposes such as (i) alerting others to your terrifying presence (ii) sounding hideous and thereby comforting to your fellow witches.

6. Make sure your Familiar keeps your means of proper travel (broomsticks) in good trim and that one, either or both of you exercise them regularly.

7. Never fail to present yourself anywhere and everywhere in full witch's uniform (i.e. black everything and no ribbons upon your hat ever). Sleeping in uniform is recommended as a means of saving dressing time.

8. Keep your Familiar happy with a good supply of Comfrey and Slime Buns. Remember, behind every great witch is a well-fed Familiar.

9. At all times acknowledge the authority of your local High Hags. As their eyes can do 360 degrees and they know everything there is to know, it is always in your interests to make their wishes your commands.

CONTRACT OF SERVICE

between
WITCH HAGATHA AGATHA, Haggy Aggy for short, HA for shortest
of Thirteen Chimneys, Wizton-under-Wold

&

the Witch's Familiar,
RUMBLEWICK SPELLWACKER MORTIMER B, RB for short

It is hereby agreed that, come
FIRE, Brimstone, CAULDRONS overflowing
or ALIEN WIZARDS invading,
for the NEXT SEVEN YEARS
RB will serve HA,
obey her EVERY WHIM AND WORD and at all times assist her
in the ways of being a true and proper WITCH.

PAYMENT for services will be:
* a log basket to sleep in   * unlimited Slime Buns for breakfast
* free use of HA's broomsticks (outside of peak brooming hours)
* and a cracked mirror for luck.

PENALTY for failing in his duties will be decided on the whim of
THE HAGS ON HIGH.

SIGNED AND SEALED
this New Moon Day, 22nd of Remember

Haggy Aggy
....
Witch Hagatha Agatha

Rumblewick
....
Rumblewick Spellwacker Mortimer B

Trixie Fiddlestick
....
And witnessed by the High Hag, Trixie Fiddlestick

ORCHARD BOOKS

338 Euston Road, London NW1 3BH
Orchard Books Australia
Level 17/207 Kent Street, Sydney NSW 2000

ISBN: 978 1 84616 072 1

First published in 2008 by Orchard Books

A CIP catalogue record for this book is

available from the British Library.

Orchard Books is a division
of Hachette Children's Books

1 3 5 7 9 10 8 6 4 2
Printed in China/Hong Kong

To my starriest-spangled
sister, Norn, with thanks
H.O.

For Leo
S.W.

Dear Precious Children

The Publisher asked me to say something about these Diaries.
(As I do not write Otherside very well, I have dictated it to
the Publisher's Familiar/assistant. If she has not written it
down right, let me know and I'll turn her into a fat pumpkin.)

This is my message: I went to a lot of trouble to steal these
Diaries for you. And the Publisher gave me a lot of shoes in
exchange. If you do not read them the Publisher may want the
shoes back. So please, for my sake — the only witch in
witchdom who isn't willing to scare you for her own
entertainment — ENJOY THEM ALL.
Yours ever,

Your fantabulous shoe-loving friend,
Hagatha Agatha (Haggy Aggy for short, HA for shortest) xx

ISBN 9781846160653

ISBN 9781846160691

ISBN 9781846160721

ISBN 9781846160714

ISBN 9781846160677

ISBN 9781846160660

ISBN 9781846160707

ISBN 9781846160684